For Breanna and Ben, the love cats.
—S. C.

For Mom and Dad. Thank you for
always taking in the strays.
—H. M.

FAMILIUS

Published by Familius LLC, www.familius.com

Familius books are available at special discounts for bulk purchases, whether for sales
promotions or for family or corporate use. For more information, contact Familius Sales at
559-876-2170 or email orders@familius.com.

Library of Congress Cataloging-in-Publication Data

2018937160   ISBN 9781641700405   eISBN 9781641700900

Edited by Brooke Jorden

Cover and book design by David Miles

Printed in China

10 9 8 7 6 5 4 3 2 1

First Edition

LUIS

AND

TABITHA

Stephanie Campisi

ILLUSTRATIONS BY

Hollie Mengert

Luis was a cat about town.

Dashing.

Charming.

Purrfectly suave.

He lived (unofficially) at the fire station and had since a daring rescue involving a very small Luis, a very shrill smoke alarm, and a very tall house. His tail still had the scorch marks.

Luis liked to go visiting, as society cats do.
Sometimes he'd travel in the fire truck.
Everywhere he went, Luis was welcomed
with open arms and leftovers.

One night, after too much catnip and too many sardines,
Luis was making his rounds when he took a wrong turn.

He climbed a wall.
And saw Tabitha.
Elegant. Silky.
Purrfectly sophisticated.

Luis stopped.

Tabitha stared.

It was love.
Love from afar.
Love under the spotlight of the moon.

Love thwarted by a thick glass door.

And by Tabitha's owner.

"Shoo!" she cried. "Shoo!"
Luis shooed, but he
wasn't done.

The next morning, Tabitha stared out at a vast bouquet of sardine tins and twine and feathers.

Luis smiled.

Tabitha smiled.

Tabitha's owner
did not smile.

"Shoo!" she cried. "Shoo!"
Luis shooed, but he wasn't done.

The next day,
he brought mice.

The day after that,
he brought pigeons.

And after that, balloons (which is not easy when you're a cat).

Each day, Luis and Tabitha stared
into each other's eyes until
Tabitha's owner chased Luis away.

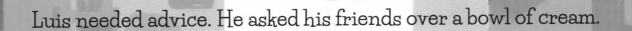

Luis needed advice. He asked his friends over a bowl of cream.

"You're an outside cat," said Mr. Pickles.

"And you need to be an inside cat," said Socks.

"Or at least look like one," said One-Eyed Winky.

Luis had an idea.

The next day, Luis showed up at Tabitha's door once more.

Luis smiled. Tabitha smiled. Tabitha's owner clutched
her hands to her heart and opened the door.

Luis was inside. Where everything was soft and warm and scratchable.

And Luis and Tabitha were inseparable.

Until the
doorbell rang.

"Is this him?"
"That's him."

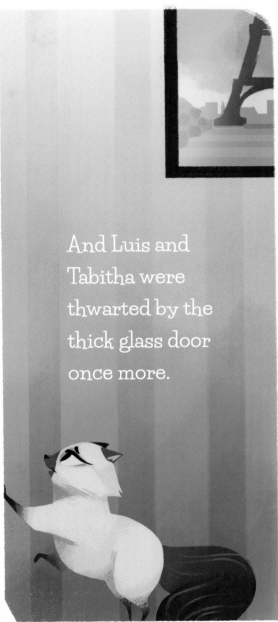

And Luis and
Tabitha were
thwarted by the
thick glass door
once more.

Luis had a new home and a new
name and a new owner . . .

. . . and all the sardines and cheese he could eat.

But all he wanted was Tabitha.
And all Tabitha wanted was Luis.

It was love. Love from afar.
Love from far too afar.

Then the doorbell rang.

"Is this him?"

"That's him. And that's *not* him."

And Luis was a
cat about town
once more.

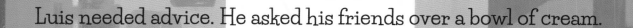

Luis needed advice. He asked his friends over a bowl of cream.

"You're an outside cat," said Mr. Pickles.

"And she's an inside cat," said Socks.

"And that's just the way it is," said One-Eyed Winky.

So Luis went visiting,
as society cats do.
He went visiting all
across town.

Everywhere he went, he was welcomed
with open arms and leftovers.

And everywhere he went, Tabitha wasn't. Until . . .

One night, Luis was riding in the fire
truck when his tail began to tingle.

Luis saw Tabitha. Elegant. Silky. *Purrfectly* sophisticated.

And in terrible danger.

The sirens began to wail. "Everyone outside!" cried the firefighters.

The crowd was a cloud of arms and shrieks as it gathered on the corner. But there was no Tabitha.

And suddenly, there was no Luis.

The crowd waited.
And worried.
And fretted.

Finally, the gray parted, and from it emerged
Luis and Tabitha, leading Tabitha's owner.
The crowd cheered.

Tabitha's owner plopped down on the curb
and clutched her hands to her heart.
She looked at Luis and Tabitha.

And smiled.

The cat show judge placed a blue ribbon on Tabitha, and the firefighters placed a gold medal on Luis and declared them both *purrfectly* heroic.

Luis was back inside.
Where everything was soft and
warm and scratchable.

And Luis and Tabitha
were inseparable.